MATTHEW WOLF

LEGENDS

A RONIN SAGA SHORT STORY

LEGENDS
A Ronin Saga Short Story
Matthew Wolf

Learn more at www.matt-wolf.com

MATTHEW WOLF

LEGENDS

A RONIN SAGA SHORT STORY

CONTENTS

LEGENDS

362 D.L.
362 Years into the Lieon, The Great War, the Last True
Council

KAIL FELT THE CRUST OF BLOOD crack and flake off of him as they stormed through the halls in the city of wind. With every step his pace quickened to the council's chambers. They had been betrayed. But they would find the culprit and seek their vengeance, or all the world would fall.

Flanking him were the other Ronin. Eight heroes who echoed his urgency. As always, Omni, Ronin of sun, and Maris, Ronin of leaf, were the nearest two—his closest companions. The others were not far behind. Water, fire, stone, moon, sun, leaf, metal, flesh. Together including him, they were the nine elemental guardians of the world and the supposed protectors of Farhaven. Yet here they were, destined to fail mankind in its final hour.

Kail wouldn't let it end this way...

As they moved, guards, servants, and couriers stared at their bloodied clothes and pressed against the wall as they passed, watching them like angels of death.

On his right, the dawning sun shone through the column of pillars. The hallway was open to the elements, revealing a city to rival all cities—the legendary Morrow, city of wind. Clouds floated by, and he caught glimpses of the rest of the city: dozens of behemoth floating rocks suspended in midair by rising winds. Each held a tiny city, connected by elaborate bridges. On each floating rock and adorning the cityscape were thousands of windmills utilizing the ever-present gusts to power the Great Kingdom.

1

Even from here, Kail felt it... the wind. It rushed up from all angles, flowing over the columns and rising like tiny white snakes vanishing into the air. If anyone peered down into that rushing wind, they would see the giant updrafts of air supported a thing of miracles—whole cities, floating on islands of rock, suspended in midair by the rising winds.

But despite the wind that spiked his senses, feeding his ire and power—the grandeur of the Great Kingdom was far from his mind.

They reached the council chamber's metal-strapped doors flanked by two hulking guards. The guards moved for the handles. Kail didn't slow. He nodded to Baro, the giant Ronin of Metal. An arsenal of weapons bristled from Baro's hulking frame. It was truly a sight, even from one legend to another. Heavy armor adorned the man from head to toe. Plate upon his arms, legs, dark metal rivets of forged from Yronia on his joints. At any seeming crack, was a thin veneer of scale mail, tiny bright metal plates. There was not an inch of the man, aside from his face, that wasn't covered in metal. Though his weapons was what made most balk in fear.

Baro bore two swords on his back, hammers, daggers, a spiked morningstar, and even a metal crossbow peaked above his shoulder. Each he had mastered, making mortal men who trained for years with blade or bow seem sluggish and awkward by comparison. At Kail's gesture, Baro grunted in affirmation and raised a hand. Immediately, threading the flow, the metal hinges sizzled and fell into molten puddles making the heavy doors groan, now unsupported. Without slowing, Kail whisked a finger and summoned his own power of the flow, the essence of all life and the power of the Ronin.

Each had their strengths: Omni's sun had vast, devastating force and accuracy, Aurelious' flesh for its healing abilities and unique conjuration, Aundevoria's stone for its protection, Seth's fire for its unbridled, wanton destruction, Dared's moon for its stealth and guile, Hiron's water for its creative applications, Maris' leaf for its cunning and power to restore the lands, Baro's metal for its talent at dissolving the world of man's creations, and for his skill with a blade. Yet wind was something else.

As wind and air were everywhere, Kail was the most powerful of all.

The flick of his finger was more than enough. A colossal surge of air smashed into the door, sending it sprawling across the marble floor. "Ah, good, I never understood why that door was there anyway," Maris remarked as the nine Ronin stepped over it, and slid past the guards who cowered against the wall.

As they entered the chambers, heated voices cut short, fancifully dressed men and women turned from a stone slab piled high with maps.

Inside, if he cared for such things, he would have gawked at the grandeur of the chambers. The Hall of Wind was breathtaking.

A large round floor was where the assembly stood. Ringing them was a series of nine round pedestals, topped by glass cases hard as steel. Each of the cases held one of the nine stones. Water, moon, stone, metal, flesh—they swirled with power and their respective element, but none dare touch them. The stones, powerful relics kept under lock and key upon penalty of death at all times, were perhaps the only objects they had kept away from the dark legions.

Aside from the stones, thick pillars held up an arched ceiling carved with an elaborate scene. Kail knew the fresco. He had even seen it commissioned on his seven-hundred and eighth birthday. It was the Legend of the Ronin, their origin, as told by the city of wind. It was just a story—each Great Kingdom had built their own over the long years. Yet he couldn't deny the image was wondrous.

The painting's central figure depicted a wizened old man descending on a glowing cloud. Nine others were beside him. Silver and gold clouds roiled as if the very heavens were their entourage. The wizened old man was God, or what man thought of as God. *He* had other names too. Among them were: the Creator, Lightbringer, Waterbringer, Master or Mistress of Shadows, Windbringer, The Great Spirit, and more. Each Great Kingdom had their own story for the origin of the Ronin. At their heart, they were the same. Each told of a figure leading nine apostles, or demi-gods, to the world of mortals to save humanity from itself. Yet the image was wrong. Kail wasn't a demigod, nor was he immortal, and most undeniably, he could not save mankind.

Beyond the pillars was an impossible drop. With no walls, the room known as the Hall of Wind seemed perched upon a cloud, overlooking the world. The air was thin and hard to breathe. They were too high for most birds to fly. For a moment, his ire waned, in a strange reverie... As if consumed by a thought that wasn't his own, and yet it was... *Birds.* Kail had always marveled at birds and their power of flight. They, above all, were light and free. *Boundless, even,* he thought enviously. Often he wondered what it would take to fly. Despite nearly a thousand years of life and the ability to wield one of the nine great elements, no thread he had ever woven could accomplish the feat. To attempt it truly would require a death wish, a desire to end it all and see what waited on the other side.

"What's the meaning of this?" a dignitary questioned.

As if dunked into a frozen lake, Kail returned to the world and the Hall of Wind. Not again, he thought... Those reveries, his strange tangential thoughts, they were happening more and more. He even realized his wrathful expression had been replaced by a... smile?

Kail felt the air tremble as several of the Ronin embraced their power. He raised a hand and they relinquished the flow, if reluctantly. *Patience,* he ordered. *We will find the betrayer and the truth soon enough.* Again, he avoided touching an item in his pocket.

"What in the seven hells of Remwar happened?" A man's voice boomed.

Fendary, the High General of their legions, rounded the stone slab, his grand cloak fluttering behind him. With his grizzled beard, deep crow's feet, and streaks of gray in his dark hair, the High General was almost ordinary looking—to a fool. Those piercing brown eyes had seen more battles in a lifetime than any one man. Fendary was the most brilliant tactician the age had ever known.

Kail knew what the assembly was gazing at, where their shocked eyes fell.

A woman screamed, and others put hands to their mouth's in terror, gazing at the newcomers in horror. Blood caked each Ronin's body. It coated their cloaks and made their hair into sticky strands with dark red clumps. In contrast, the monarchs and emissaries before them were immaculately dressed. Fine cloth and silk draped their bodies. By comparison, the Ronin looked like demons.

"You do realize a bath is still a tradition in this age, Ronin? Even a butcher cleans after he performs his duty." The woman who spoke wrinkled her nose, as if not so much disgusted by the blood, but by their lack of decorum. Standing in an elegant purple dress, Queen Ophelia was as stunning as ever. Queen of the City of Covai, the Kingdom of Flesh, Ophelia was strikingly beautiful—even to Kail's hardened heart—with fiery hair and dark olive skin. Her dress was less than modest with a plunging neckline that exposed her amble curves. Kail had seen her type before, those that used their bodies as weapons. But there was something in her eyes— something that said she was both curious and afraid by his blood stained skin.

A man in red robes with four stripes on his cuff strode forward. Reaver Nevar was an ambassador of the Citadel, the Great Kingdom of Fire. The red robes of a Reaver and the four stripes of rank attested to his power. "What's the meaning of this spectacle? Why are you here when we sent you to the Frizzian Coast?"

Seth broke rank and strode forward. He grabbed Reaver Never by his collar and raised him into the air. Flames danced in the Ronin of fire's eyes as he growled, "Because, my little spark wielding friend, you didn't send us to the coast. You sent us to our *death*. Or at least... you tried."

"Let me go!" the man cursed. Fire swirled around Reaver Nevar's hand. The Reaver cast out a hand, sending angry red flames curling around Seth's form, turning the Ronin of fire into a living torch.

Kail didn't move a muscle.

Through firestorm, Seth laughed. Nevar's eyes grew wide with surprise, pouring in more of his power. Seth clamped a hand over the Reaver's fist. At once, the flames in the room were snuffed like a blanket over a campfire. Despite the inferno, the only sign of the Reaver's attack were faint, curling wisps of smoke. Seth patted the smoking bits of clothing casually with his free hand, putting them out. "Fire? Are you an imbecile?" Seth sniffed contemptuously. "Let me show you what true fire looks like." A dark amber glow grew around Seth. Flames singed, burning away Reaver Nevar's scarlet robes. The man began to scream.

"Enough," Kail ordered. "Drop him."

It's him, Kail. Seth thought angrily. *He's the traitor. I know it!* The air in the room grew stifling as fire danced in Seth's eyes.

Release him, brother, Kail commanded through the link.

Omni, ever the light of reason, echoed his words, *You've impressed upon them the importance of our arrival, Seth, but now let him go.* It was true. Kail turned to see the terrified faces of the dignitaries—men and women who had seen the atrocities of this war.

Seth growled and dropped Reaver Nevar who shook on the ground, eyeing the missing sleeves of his scarlet robes and his arms reddened by the instant flames.

Accusing the counsel... This will break us, Maris said through the bond. *Are we certain about this? There's no going back.*

We are already broken, Omni replied. *At least we'll know the truth.* Then, her bright blue eyes solemn, she nodded, encouraging him to continue.

Kail spoke again, "As were our orders, we headed to the Frizzian Coast to aid in the ongoing war on the Plains of Aster. When we arrived, the battle was quickly turning in favor of the Alliance. We were losing. Saeroks and vergs were everywhere, and nameless outnumbered us two to one. Finally, after days of bloodshed and death, we turned the tide and the Alliance broke and fled. We thought we had won." He laughed at that, though it hurt to do so.

"Where did you go?" King Gias, ruler of Eldas home of the elves, questioned.

"To the only shelter we knew. We gathered our wounded and traveled to the City of Gal. That was our plan at least..." Kail's mind flashed back.

He saw the lone stretch of road. The night was silent, aside from the soft clop of hooves and the rattle of armor. The orange glow of paper lanterns was the only light in an otherwise black night. They glimpsed the city's stone walls in the distance through a last stand of trees. Whispers of

*relief sifted through the army. Suddenly, a howl pierced the air. Battle
cries shook the night as they were attacked from all sides.*

"We were ambushed," he said. "Within sight of the city walls of Gal, the
enemy sprung their trap." Instead of the gold-veined marble beneath him,
Kail saw the bodies once again. The dead were everywhere, piling towards
the ceiling. They gasped and coughed blood, reaching for him, but there
was nothing he could do—just like back then. Not even Aurelious' powers
of knitting flesh could save a man from a nameless' cruel blade.

Fendary gripped his shoulder breaking him from his trance. "How
many?"

Kail's fist clenched around Morrowil's handle, dried blood flaking from
his hand. He wasn't sure when he had unsheathed the blade. "We were the
only survivors," he answered.

"Where was Gal in all this?" another questioned.

Kail's hand tightened on Morrowil. Something felt different about the
blade. "We wondered the same, so we brought down the doors of the city.
What we saw... It was a graveyard. A ghost town filled with only broken
buildings and dead bodies."

"What about Governor Jacek and the Assembly?" King Gias asked.

"We found them in the throne room, all slaughtered or worse."

"Worse? What do you mean?" Ophelia asked.

Reaver Nevar quivered in anger, face reddening to match his crimson
beard. "You're wrong! A hundred thousand men were stationed in that city.
There's no way it could have fallen!"

Shall I? Dared, the silent Ronin asked.

Kail nodded.

The man rose from the shadows. With his dagger he cut the cords of a
wrapped bundle and rolled the parcel into the center of the room. Kail
issued filaments of wind. The cloth was pushed aside to reveal a severed
head.

A servant holding a silver pitcher screamed, and dropped the pitcher,
stepping back to the corner of the room. More dignitaries gasped, but many
simply stared in disbelief. The head gazed back, mouth agape, lips slack,

and eyes rimmed with blood. The dead man's black hair was oiled and slick against his pate, and a huge gash ran down the center, as if a blunt axe had failed to cleave his thick skull. Worst of all, his ears, nose, and most of his neck appeared masticated from a hungry verg or saerok. Aurelious had kept the head fresh with strands of flesh. As a result, the dead man's lips twitched or eyes rolled occasionally as the threads made the muscles move, preventing atrophy and decay.

"Governor Jacek," King Gias breathed.

Governor Jacek's upper lip trembled as if in reply. An ambassador vomited on the ground. Reaver Nevar put a hand to his mouth, turning, while Queen Ophelia blanched. The rest of the dignitariesstepped back. All but Fendary.

The High General's hand swiped across the slab, throwing maps upon the ground. "The Alliance," he growled. "Those bastards. By the gods, they'll pay for this."

"Ah, but you have not heard the best part," Kail twirled Morrowil in his hands as he circled them, footsteps falling upon the smooth white marble. The dignitaries watched as he moved through the pillars.

Queen Ophelia waved a hand. The sobbing serving girl recognized the dismissal and fled the chambers through the open door. "Congratulations. You've scared the serving girl thoroughly with your little parlor trick. Now stop baiting us and speak straightly."

"The truth was in the dead. Judging by the decay, the city and its inhabitants had been dead for nearly two moons."

"What are you trying to say?" Another emissary asked.

"Two moons..." King Gias spoke, as if realizing before the others. "Two months..."

Kail sighed. "Isn't it obvious? The city had been gutted long before we got there."

"But the reports..." Fendary said, shaking his head.

Kail spat the next words, walking a line before the richly clothed dignitaries. "We've been fed lies. Fattened like hogs for the slaughter with misinformation, leading us to this moment. We gathered the majority of our forces in one place, and they took it long ago. They burned and died, meanwhile we were fed reports for trivial battles in far-flung places."

Maris added, "Played like a fools right into the hand of the dealer. Playing cards while he held the whole deck behind the table. Fighting pointless battles in the east and south while our main force in Gal waged a terrible war. Those poor bastards... they must've wondered why and where we were..."

"It can't be," Reaver Nevar whisper, still sitting the ground, shaking his head. "Gal..."

"Is gone," Kail finished. "Whoever betrayed us, has been pulling our strings for weeks, months now. We lost a long time ago, and we didn't even know it. We are all that's left."

Fendary stared at the masticated head in disbelief. "How? Who would betray us?"

Kail raised his blade pointing to the dignitaries.

Queen Ophelia touched something under the cover of her dress as if for reassurance, hidden beneath her neckline.

"It's simple. Since the order and reports came from this room, the betrayer stands among us."

Shouts and questions made the room ring.

"*Silence!*" His voice boomed, tousling hair and cloak. A thunderclap of wind burst from his center and knocked the council to the ground. He pressed the air around them, freezing them in place.

Reaver Nevar cried, "Let us go! You're mad!" He cast bouts of fire trying to sever his bonds, but despite the man's skill it was no match for Kail. No one was a match for him.

Queen Ophelia shrieked with fury, "The Ronin are sworn to be weapons against only the enemy! You break the code by fighting us and shall lose your role as peacekeepers!"

Kail listened, hesitating. It was true. For nearly a thousand years, the Ronin were known as peacekeepers. War torn cities, feuding tribes, or a rebel monarch, all put down their blades and found peace in the presence of the Ronin. He weighed her words and spoke at last, turning his back, "Sometimes to create peace you must use force. We are that force."

Several cried out and he wove more strands, cramming balls of air in their mouths, silencing them. Calmly, he walked to the edge of the room, and stood on the lip. He felt the wind of the heights flowing over him, giving him power and life. It also provided clarity. Over the years he had gazed upon it many times, eyeing the city that hugged the steep walls, for all of Morrow sat upon the windy cliffs of Ren Nar. He thought of the people, and heardthe ring of the blacksmiths' hammers with the rising dawn. Long ago the song of war had replaced the normal hum of life.

Morrow was his home and he would not let it fall, not if he had to kill a thousand betrayers. As he paused, a harsh truth wormed its way into his thoughts. He knew the Alliance would simply send another traitor, another person to kill in this endless war. What would it take to end it all? Whatever it was, had he not already given everything? Yet still he knew, he would gladly give more—anything to see an end to the ceaseless death and destruction.

Kail looked back at his friends—the Ronin.

Sun. Leaf. Water. Fire. Stone. Moon. Flesh. Metal.

What now? Maris asked, picking a splinter of wood from his hair.

How do we reveal the betrayer? Dared echoed from the shadows.

And what if there's more than one? Baro asked.

Seth fumed, striding forward. "Then we will flush them all out, torturing them one at a time," he said aloud. Through the ki, power of the Devari and an ability to sense another emotions, Kail felt the dignitaries' fear spike.

When did you lose your mind, Seth? Maris replied. *We cannot abandon reason.*

And what is one life weighed against thousands, Maris? Aurelious said.

Every life is important, brother, Aundevoria countered.

Ragefire, that terrible flame, danced in Seth's palm. *If none of you have the stomach for it then—*

Silence, Kail said. The ragefire was vanquished by a gust of wind. *The fool,* while it wasn't as hot as Omni's power of sun, ragefire was true to its name, consuming and spreading to everything it touched. Even the smallest bit of ragefire would incinerate everything in the room. Kail was tired. Worn from the same, endless arguments. Long ago he realized each Ronin held an unrelenting personality that matched their elements. Hiron was cool as water, Omni provided the light of wisdom, Seth the fire of passion, and so on—and as a result a balance was created, mimicking the duality of life. At that moment, it tired him, and knew it was going nowhere. He sighed, turning away from the impossible drop and back to the golden hall when Fendary stepped up and in his way.

"Step aside, friend," Kail ordered.

Fendary stood straight. "No."

"So be it," Kail nodded and Baro and Maris dragged the general aside.

"Let me go!" Fen growled.

With the High General out of the way, Kail raised his arm, lifting the other dignitaries into the air. A chorus of confusion echoed from the esteemed men and women.

Fendary's voice cut through the rabble, "What in the seven hells of Remwar do you think you're doing, Kail? This is reckless and brash, even for you!"

"I do only what is necessary, old friend. You fear dissension, but it's already upon us. You speak about holding onto something, but what is there left to hold onto?"

"This," Fendary howled, held by the two Ronin, nodding to the hanging dignitaries, "this is what they want. Suspicion and doubt. What need is there to fight us, if we tear ourselves apart?"

Kail knew he was right and yet... "Tell me, old friend, how long and hard have we fought together."

"Too long," Fen said quietly.

Kail had known Fendary all his life—since the veteran was a toddler hiding behind his mother's skirts. Kail had watched that small boy become a young man. Had trained with Fendary and had been his first sparring partner. Had then seen the young man's zeal tempered with age and experience, become a grown man. The years had passed, and now Fendary was the grizzled veteran that stood before him. Fendary's many years had worn on him like a battered sword, weathered and chipped. While the High General was a fraction of Kail's age, with his gray hair and deep set wrinkles, Fendary could have passed for his grandfather. However, if Kail were to have a soft spot for any man in this room aside from his fellow Ronin, it would be for the High General.

"And in all that time," Kail posed, "have I ever questioned your orders or the decisions of this council? I have nearly died a thousand deaths for Farhaven, for what some may call the greater good. I... I've watched more friends and lovers die within my arms than a hundred men. We all have," he said, looking to the other Ronin. So many years and so much loss. For what? Greed knew no bounds, and the war that had begun so long ago seemed to bleed Farhaven dry. Hope. He'd clung to that word, to the memory of peace, but now peace in wartime was like a distant memory. A laughable notion only the naive or mad still clung to. His last words broke his voice slightly, giving it a hitch, but he trudged onward. "In the end, we've done everything you and this council have asked us—our lives, our very *souls* are yours—and what do we get? This—" he pointed to the masticated head of Governor Jacek. "We've been lied to. You've been lied to, my friend. We've been fighting a battle beyond our walls, but the true enemy is inside, among us all along."

"Then we discuss this rationally, we find the traitor and bring order to our cause—"

"—Our *cause*?" Kail laughed, and it had a maddening tone to it. "What cause is there? We had armies. We don't anymore. All our hopes, our forces lay in Gal, which is now a corpse of a city. Now all we have left is us, and a smattering of boys that lie within these walls, too young to hold their father's blades. Our cause is dead. Humanity is gone."

Fendary's jaw tightened. "It is not gone yet... There are still the Gates."

"The Gates?" Kail laughed. "They are far from built. You rest your hopes on a fool's errand."

King Gias, the leader of Eldas, and elven king struggled in his bonds. Kail lifted a hand, and released the threads of air filling his mouth. Gias

12

spoke, "Hope is not gone, Kail. Listen to me.... The Gates, they will be finished."

"Even if they are, the shadow is too strong," Aurelious, Ronin of Flesh, echoed. Kail knew what he meant... The Kage, often called the Shadow. Nine creatures that looked like each of the Ronin and mirrored their powers, but were made by dark magic, no one knew from where they had come, but they had spawned a thousand years ago. With them came the rise of other nightmarish creatures, vergs, monstrous like trolls with thick leathery hide, saeroks, fox-faced, lanky werewolf-like beasts with mangy furred bodies, and dagger-length claws, and nameless, the captains of the dark legions. Rumors said nameless had once been Reavers who had sacrificed themselves to their cause, and been made into something unholy. Black-cloaked warriors, nameless could shift a killing blow by turning into dark mist, and then reappear a dozen feet away. But the Kage were something else, something much worse.

Kail had seen the Kage up close. Nine warriors. Each could thread the nine elements: a dark Seth, Maris, Omni, Aurelious, Aundevoria, Baro, Dared, Hiron, and even one for him, a dark leader. They wore similar clothes that matched their element and color, but that is where the resemblance ended. A Kage's skin was ghostly white like a corpse's flesh, rotting in places, showing red exposed muscle and sinew. An awful smell emanated from them even from a distance, and he'd seen maggots crawling out of their clothes.

That was how the war had started—by the nine creatures posing as them, discrediting their deeds and sowing evil. At first, the Kage had looked the same. A mirror image. Spreading the evil perception that the Ronin had betrayed everyone. Over time, however, their spell had begun to decay, exposing their true nature and the demons beneath.

Now the distinction between the two—Ronin and Kage, reality and shadow, no longer seemed to matter. The dark army had grown. The leaders of the Alliance—those still human—seemed controlled, manipulated by some dark magic that nothing but death could dissolve.

13

Aurelious continued, "They are us, but with a dark army at their heels, an endless supply of creatures to throw at us and wear us down until we are no more."

King Gias smiled, his sprig-green eyes full of confidence. "The Gates will stop them. Bound by the magic of sacrifice, it will work."

It had been an idea borne out of sheer impossible hope. An idea to trap the Kage and their armies in the lands to the south behind a Gate made of magic. In ancient books, there had been powerful spells that suggested a land could be purged of its magic. Left behind the Gates, the hope was the magic-less land would starve the nightmares and their horde, and kill them slowly. *Spark dead* would be the land's name, or 'Daerval' in the old tongue. But it was an ambitious project. A faint hope with little chance of success. They'd been building the Gates for months while men clashed and died. Truthfully, Kail had forgotten about the Gates until now. Banished it from his mind, knowing it was a plan they didn't dare pin their hopes on, in fear of losing all faith if it failed.

Maybe it can work. Maybe we can stop them, Aundevoria thought through their bond, his stony exterior cracking and exposing his ever-present belief in the power of humanity.

Big Baro, Ronin of Metal spoke, "But who will drag them there? Someone has to act as bait to bring the shadow to the land without magic and be trapped alongside them. Who would be willing to sacrifice themselves with no hope for survival?"

Then the Ronin that never spoke, gave voice to the truth they were all thinking. In a gravely low tone that surprised even Kail, Dared, Ronin of Moon, said, "We will."

"Then what? We will be trapped against the Gates in a land without magic," Aurelious, Ronin of Flesh, said.

The dark silence of what was obvious hung in the air until the Ronin of Fire spoke. "What do you think? Then we die," Seth said with a bemused smile, a fire dancing in his eyes.

"Die and let the rest of humanity live," Aundevoria said, nodding as if Seth was speaking a great truth.

The rest looked thoughtful. Kail felt hope flicker in his friends through their bond. *Sacrificial pawns to the very end. Is that all they were?*

"How close are you to being done with the Gates?" Omni, Ronin of Sun, asked.

"Days," King Gias answered, "maybe a week at most. My elves work on the Gates day and night without sleep. With the help of the Untamed we have gathered, and those who have pledged to give their lives to seal it, we will finish."

Baro grumbled, "I never thought we'd win this war, but we may stop them after all... Maybe he's right, Kail. Maybe there's still hope."

"No," Kail said quietly. "There's no hope while a traitor lies in our midst. They'll destroy the Gates and any hope we have with it." Silence settled as all eyes turned to the suspects of the betrayal. The dignitaries still hung in the air by threads of wind. Most looked indignant, some terrified with sweat running down their temples or wide fearful eyes, but all were unwilling spectators to their impending trial and conviction. "We must find the culprit and put an end to it." Fendary still stood in Kail's way. "So face me now, old friend, or stand aside and let me do what I must do," he swore, feeling a fire behind his own eyes as he stared at his long-time friend.

Cursing, the High General stepped aside.

Kail lowered the dignitaries until their feet dangled just above the floor. He raised Morrowil, walking slowly, gripping the smooth item in his pocket. He let the anger of the object fill him like a fount of wrath. Morrowil's tip brushed their necks and they stirred, most trembling or trying to pull away. Then he paused at Reaver Nevar. Kail cocked his head and stared into the man's eyes. He saw fire as well as fear, but nothing more. The dark glint of guilt was absent from the man's gaze. He continued and Nevar sagged. Kail slowed when he reached Queen Ophelia. The blade lingered at the hollow of her throat.

The woman's face was curiously blank, not even a flicker of fear.

He released the bonds of wind in her mouth. "Speak. If you are innocent, let us hear it."

15

"And why should I? You've the look of a man who thinks he can play god. There is no truth, no justice here. You will only twist my words to see what you wish to seek—all to slake your thirst for vengeance."

"You're wrong. I can sense your truth, dear queen. I have the ki." The ki was the Devari power of empathy—and Kail, as the Leader of the Devari, wielded it more fully than any other.

"So?" Ophelia asked, a twist of condescension on her pretty red lips, her eyes still haughty and filled with a clever light. "All you can sense is my terror or my indifference. Neither speaks to my guilt."

"You'd be surprised. The fear of death is a powerful motivator. It has a tendency to flush out the truth," Kail said calmly. Morrowil hovered closer to her throat.

"Or make me lie in hope to save my life."

"Lying would be a mistake," he answered. "I can sense that too."

The Queen of Flesh raised a pious eyebrow. "Your scare tactics won't work on me, Ronin." Kail hesitated, Morrowil's tip stopping its bite at her throat. "I see the light in your eyes, the feeling of righteous judgement. But there is nothing righteous here. Only a man blinded by his impotent rage. Any truth you gain will be truth pried by force, and will be worthless and you know it."

Kail ignored her clever tirade. Beneath the surface, he sensed... something in Ophelia. Something she was hiding. Ophelia swallowed and Morrowil nicked her smooth skin, creating a thin line of blood. "I've done nothing wrong," she said, suddenly more panicked. Her mask of confidence was cracking.

Kail took the smooth item from his pocket. "Is that so? We found this in the throne room of Gal, amid the dead," he announced and held the object high so all could see. A piece of ruby glittered as light flowed through its facets. It cast shades of blood red on all the dignitaries. "Did you know," he asked her, "we have a tendency to touch things we hold dear when we are nervous... even things that might incriminate us." Now he felt Ophelia's fear spike through the ki. The beautiful queen's face flushed with true panic for the first time, eyes splitting wide. Kail smiled sadly. "A shame really, that we can be the product of our own downfall."

He stepped forward.

"Stay back," she growled, trying to twist away from his outstretched finger.

"Don't worry, you're not my type." Locking her in place with threads of wind, Kail moved the collar of the queen's dress aside, exposing a thin gold chain.

"Enough!" Ophelia shouted, shaking her neck enough to let the gold chain fall back into the plunging neckline of her dress. "You accuse us, treat us like common thieves, yet it is you who is at fault!" her voice gained strength, "You break your code by threatening those you were sworn to protect. In the end, you are nothing more than a defective relic that doesn't know its pl—"

Kail was through with this game. He grabbed the chain, snapped it from her neck and released the threads of wind that held her, letting her collapse to the ground. He turned from her.

Ophelia screamed, lashing out. He sensed the disturbance in the air behind him, the parting of wind as she pulled a dagger and lunged at him. The eight other Ronin could have reacted, but they let him handle the nuisance. With a flick of his hand a gust of air swept her off her feet, sending her sprawling on the smooth marble.

Calmly, he eyed the amulet in his hand, admiring the fine gold setting cast into the symbol of flesh.

A ruby in the amulet matched the one in his hand. Holding it to the sun, he pressed the matching ruby beside its twin. It clicked into place.

Queen Ophelia staggered to her feet.

This time, Aurelious, Ronin of flesh raised his hand. Kail saw the woman freeze in place—her every muscle tensed, her body going rigid as if lightning raced through her body. Tendons stood out starkly in her neck, making her look much more like the monster she truly was.

"It seems we've found the owner, my queen," he said.

Ophelia quivered, rooted by Aurelious' threads of flesh. She twitched, craning her neck to look at the brown-haired Ronin of flesh whose fingers and eyes danced with power. "Aurelious! What are you doing? I am your queen! I am the ruler of Covai, the Great Kingdom of Flesh—you are my servant and I order you to let me go this instant!"

Aurelious dark eyes glittered as he strode up to her, fingers still dancing, making her muscles and face twitch. "I'm disappointed. In all these years as your advisor you've never really understood me, understood us, have you? To be a Ronin means to keep the peace of this world, to bring balance. You, my queen, are a blight upon that peace." Aurelious gave a tight-lipped smile, a smile that touched his dark eyes. "I always found it funny that we were once called Kingkillers, as queens die just as easily."

As she trembled, Kail took Aurelious' place.

He grabbed her neck in one mighty grip and embraced his power. White eddies curled around his limbs. "Whom do you answer to, and what do they want?"

Ophelia closed her eyes with a bitter laugh. "What if I tell you? What then? Who's to say you will not just kill me as soon as the words leave my mouth?"

"A good question. However, if you do not answer, then you are surely choosing death."

There was the ring of steel. Kail turned to see Fendary unsheathe his broadsword. He eyed the High General and his blade; notches marred its edge, worn from countless battles. "Put down Morrowil, Kail. This is not right, and you know it. Let us show her to the world as a usurper of peace, try her of her crimes by a proper tribunal, and end her life. I cannot stand by idly and watch as you become both judge and executioner."

Kail threw an arm out. Fendary raised his blade, but threads of wind locked him in place, sword frozen as the gag of air filled the High General's mouth again. Kail felt a wave of guilt, but he suppressed it. "Continue," he growled, eyeing the queen of flesh.

Ophelia stared down her long nose through her tangle of crimson hair, "Kill me—it's pointless if I tell you anyway. There's no hope left for this world."

"Is that why you betrayed us? Your cowardice is our downfall."

"There's a fine line between a coward and a plain fool," she said, eyes bloodshot with rage, "Besides... You don't know what they have on me... What they stole from me... If I do this, then, maybe... maybe they will hold to their bargain."

"You sacrificed the world for one person?"

Ophelia shook her head. "You don't understand. She..." he voice hitched, tears forming in her eyes, "she is everything to me."

Maris cackled, a maddening laugh, pulling his hands through his hair. "Gods, we were betrayed for the sake of a mother's lunacy. Farhaven falls because of a single girl? Are you insane?"

Ophelia only glared at him, then looked away.

"You cannot argue with the heart," Omni said. "Even when that heart is possessed by a self-serving dimwit."

Ophelia sneered at Omni. "What do you know? We're all doomed anyway. You think I am the reason for our end? Then you are the imbecile. They could end us anytime. I am just a cog, an insect in their greater plans.

Now, the wise ones save what they can. When a fox is caught in a trap, it doesn't hope and pray, it gnaws its leg and finds a way out."

"A selfish coward's excuse," Aundevoria said. "There is always hope."

"You're delusional. You all are," Ophelia said, laughing, "Look at that map and see for yourself! We are outnumbered a thousand to one. We are on the cusp of defeat. The last thing standing in the Alliances' way is Morrow. Floating cities or high walls won't stop them, Ronin. You cannot escape their reach. This city will not last against the might of the Alliance. They will throw their dark armies upon you—legions of vergs and saeroks. Nameless will fill the streets, striking terror into the hearts of these *free* people." She laughed. "At their head, the Kage will make the city tremble."

With a hand of wind, Kail struck her across the face creating a spray of fine blood that matched her crimson hair. Her neck craned from the power of the blow. Slowly, Ophelia's gaze returned and Kail felt his heart darken. A crazed, possessed smile twisted her voluptuous lips. "You fear it, because it's true. You fear them, because they will win. There is only one sane path left now."

"And that is?" Baro questioned in his deep rumble.

"The only reasonable option is to strike a deal with the Alliance and hope for their mercy."

Omni unsheathed Sefaras, Blade of Sun, with a ring. The sword blazed with golden light. "I've heard enough. The only mercy for which you can hope is a quick death, Ophelia. It is more than a traitor like you deserves."

The mad queen hunched. Suddenly, her body shook. A depraved, throaty laugh filled the room. "You are fools. The Alliance is but a cloak, a mere shell of armor for *he* who controls it."

Kail's blood froze.

He? The other Ronin voiced as one through the bond.

"You're lying," Kail said.

"You fear something that does not exist. If you vanquished the Alliance tomorrow it would not matter. It is not even his goal. To kill you, to wipe you from this world is but a necessary step in order to gain them."

Gain... them?

20

The other Ronin looked at each other, confused. They had heard whispers of a head of the snake, of true dark purpose... But only whispers. Now it was here. Now he *had* to know.

Sheathing Morrowil upon his back, Kail grabbed her by the collar, lifting her with his own might. She struggled, clawing at his hands. Walking to the hall's edge, Kail suspended her over the endless abyss. "Who is he? What does he want? Tell me everything or enjoy your fall."

Ophelia's wide eyes stared at the sharp cliff and endless fall, body rigid with fear. "I will tell you, but it won't matter."

"Speak!"

"I... I was given orders by a man in a dark cloak, around your height. He said little, and asked even less. Yet on our last encounter, he dropped something."

"What was it?" Kail said.

Ophelia laughed again, and a darkness like fetid oil churned in the whites of her eyes.

Kail's fingers tightened around her throat. The wind around his frame spiked, thicker eddies swirling. Ophelia choked, but still her eyes mocked him. He knew there was nothing he could do to make her speak. Hope slipped through his grasp, and he squeezed harder.

Kail, enough! Hiron shouted.

We need her! Omni shouted. *You kill her, you destroy the truth!*

Ophelia's once flawless skin turned red and then purple. Her limbs shuddered, flailing as the last of her breath and life fled.

"Tell me!" he bellowed, his voice filled with the power of the wind.

Stop him, Omni ordered—a distant command.

Distantly, Kail felt the others threading. A wave of heat crashed against his back, but it dissipated against his shield of raging wind. Then, he saw a flash. Aundevoria vaulted towards him. Without thought, Kail channeled the wind that encased him. It flowed like quicksilver, engulfing his palm in layers thicker than steel. Aundevoria swung, stone sword racing. Kail caught the blade midair. As soon as he did, thick green vines sprouted from the sword and crawled over his arm. Like a serpent, the vines slithered, circling his waist. They grew, constricting his limbs until their weight made his legs buckle. He stumbled backward and Ophelia fell from his grasp, gasping for air.

The mad queen peered through her wild hair like writhing snakes. "See?" she coughed, "Even the Ronin are doomed to fail."

The vines were now thicker than his torso, pressing him flat against the stone. He felt Morrowil's presence upon his back. Wriggling a hand free, Kail gripped the blade's handle. The flow roared through his veins like a torrent until he wanted to burst. He formed threads of air, slicing the wrist-thick tubers with a thousand tiny blades and the green vines fell to pieces around him. Kail rose when big arms engulfed him like massive iron chains. Immediately, he fought back with a gust of concentrated air, but still his assailant held on. Kail took a calming breath. Using every muscle he snapped his body, thrusting his shoulder into the man's gut. The big man flew back with a grunt.

"It's done, stop!" A voice shouted. "Let him go!"

But Kail was lost in the power and rage flowing through him. He turned on them slowly. They dare attack him... His own brothers and sister. The betrayal was far deeper than he ever imagined. It felt like shards stabbing his heart, but it didn't matter. None of it mattered. With Morrowil, he was powerful enough. If he had to stop the darkness, stop the enemy, stop even his own brothers, sister, and all the armies with own hands, he would.

Kail threaded wind, terrible, mighty gusts. Flinging a hand, he grabbed those nearest in his grasp, twisting them, wringing them of life. At the same time, he sent bolts of hardened wind like invisible rocks flying through the air. Sudden fire lashed at him, but he created a wall of wind. The fire grew until all he could see were flames. Something gripped his arms and legs. Glowing golden shackles. Omni's work. She was powerful, but he was more and—

—Light filled his vision. *Kail!* A familiar voice shouted through the roar of flames. *Stop this madness!*

Omni? A voice whispered, piercing the anger that clouded his thoughts. *What am I doing?* His power waned, and thoughts returned more sluggishly.

Morrowil was in his hand. Through the flames, he saw the blade's normally silver surface now streaked with black. *Find the truth,* the blade whispered. Ophelia still lie on the ground. The betrayer. The one who had dashed all their hopes—who had led them to the edge of defeat. It was her fault and still she hid the truth from him, hid their true enemy and the perpetrator of this dark war. *The truth,* the blade whispered again, *find the truth,* even more urgent, more demanding.

Kail nodded, letting his dark rage take control once more.

Fire and light still swirled about him, locking him in place. They were strong. Gripping a reserve of power from a place of desperation, Kail unleashed several more bolts of air without looking. The fire fell, and the bonds of light dissipated.

He stepped towards Ophelia. Suddenly, the marble grew slick as ice sprouted from the ground and encased his legs. He ignored it, lifting Ophelia into the air with the flow and pressing the blade to her throat. *"Where is it? What did you find?"* Even his voice didn't sound his own. A rasping, deep and baleful snarl.

Her eyes flashed, darting to a small pouch at her waist. Kail released her and she collapsed to the ground, before looking up at him with hateful eyes. "*He* will find you, once he finds the Objects of his desire, he will—"

Kail swung Morrowil. Her words fell short as her scarlet-shrouded head rolled across the floor. Silently, he grabbed the pouch and sheathed the blade. He looked around, and the world returned once again, as if a veil had been lifted. Maps were strewn. Smoke and scorch marks from bouts of fire scarred the marbled floor.

Four Ronin—Seth, Aundevoria, Baro and Omni lay wounded. Aurelious tended Seth who bore a large gash upon his head, while Baro rubbed his ribs. The big man looked as if hit by a bull. Omni lay beside a pillar, still as death. He saw the dignitaries cowering behind a wall of ice and moon.

23

Then he saw Fendary. The High General's eyes were locked upon him, his sword still frozen by threads of wind, yet somehow in the clash he had thrown a dense bolt of wind. Now a fist-sized hole leaked blood from Fendary's chest. A fist-sized empty space just above his heart.

"Gods, no..." Confusion and anger spiraled through him. Fury filled his voice, "What happened?" He released the threads, and the High General fell to the ground, dead. Kail's breath quickened in horror.

Nearby, Maris knelt beside Omni, his clothes in tatters. His closest friend who now stared at him as if he was a monster.

In a rush, it all returned, as if waking.

Kail distantly remembered wind, fighting, fire, and rage. The general had been charging him and he had sent bolts of wind and—

"Good gods what have I done," he breathed, his soul aching. Kail looked to his closest friend in all the world. "Maris, I didn't mean, it wasn't me—" he moved to help his brother. Maris rose, raising his blade. The man often called the Trickster held no mirth on his face now. Instead, he looked ready to fight or die. Worse, he looked as if he didn't know who Kail was.

The others were the same. They all eyed him as if they no longer knew him. Kail felt another presence and he remembered, looking down. Morrowil.

The normally white wind that coursed around the blade was wholly different. An inky darkness slithered over the sword's surface. Shuddering, he hurled the blade. Morrowil clattered along the ground, and the darkness pulled back into the blade.

Then a scene, a memory, flashed in his head as if from another's eyes.

A pale moon hung in the sky, lighting the dark night. A woman strode towards him. Though her face was hidden within her deep hood, he saw ringlets of crimson peek from her cowl and a body full of seductive curves accented by the thin cloth of her baggy robes with each sway of her hips. Yet her stride held a hiccup of fear to it. She stopped before him, glancing about at the shadows as if waiting for monsters to step out of the night.

"Is it done?" he asked.

"Yes. Gal has fallen," she answered.

"Then all that remains is Morrow," he said. "The last bastion until Farhaven is ours."

"And the Ronin..." she breathed.

"The Ronin will die. The trap waits for them at Gal."

She shook her head, afraid. "The trap won't work. The Ronin can't be defeated."

"The shadow is coming for them, and even legends have their weaknesses," he answered.

"If they discover who I am," the woman said. "They will kill me. This has to be it... Swear this is it! Swear you will keep me safe!"

"Safe?" He laughed. "I tried to keep the world safe, and this..." He looked down and saw black veins pulsing like dark worms in his arm. "This is who I've become. The shadow—He—will consume everything. He will turn the world to flames, and remake it in his vision. No one is safe." He turned to leave, moving back to the shadows.

"Wait," the woman called, "Who are you at least?"

"I..." He drew a blank, until the question was snuffed as he gripped the blade tighter.

.

25

Suddenly, the blade in his hand tingled and a sharp pain shot through his arm. He held back a gasp of agony, watching as his hand shuddered uncontrollably, releasing the hilt. The blade fell to the ground.

Kail returned. Morrowil lay at his feet. In his hand, he held the leather pouch with the woven symbols of the element of flesh. Slowly, he loosened the pouch's thong and turned it over.

A small piece of metal dropped into the flat of his hand. It was a menuki, the small talisman traditionally embedded in the blade's handle. It sat between the scarlet leather grip and the gray ray skin beneath. It was worn almost beyond recognition, and yet...

Slowly, Kail picked up Morrowil. He slid the metal ornament beneath the dyed leather and into a hollow shaped like the symbol of wind.

It fit perfectly.

He knew it would. Just as he knew why his sword had felt different until now. The weight was once again familiar. It was whole, the way it had not felt since the talisman had fallen out that night. The night he had betrayed his own brothers.

He was the betrayer.

Why—how—a torrent of fear, of despair, of questions tore through him.

Kail shook his head. "No, this is impossible."

The other Ronin must have seen the small emblem as well, as they stared at him in horror. He felt their hot gazes of fear, of anger. The small metal emblem of wind that Ophelia, the traitor carried was proof beyond a shadow of doubt. Yet why would he become evil? How was that possible? And yet he knew the answer already.

Morrowil.

The blade was not evil, but it drew out the potential, the hope, the fear, the need inside a person. If that need came from a place of darkness, of hate—then so to did the power. In a desperate desire for power to end this war, Kail had pulled from a place of darkness, of hate. He'd corrupted himself.

"Morrowil," he whispered.

It was silent.

"Answer me!" Fear and anger rose inside him. The blade grew heavy in his hands, as if it were trying to drag itself from his grip. "No, not now," he swore, "You cannot abandon me." He gripped it with both hands and searing pain crawled up his arms. Kail grit his teeth, fighting off the agony. He'd heard of such a thing and knew.

Its message was clear—Morrowil sought a new owner. He had pulled on it too greedily, too desperately to save the world and it had been his downfall. It had been all their downfall... And yet... there was only one reason the blade was growing heavy. Why it hurt to touch. It wasn't his anymore. Realization dawned on him through the agony of what he'd just done. Was that it? Were the Ronin broken because of him?

No... If Morrowil sought a new owner, that meant...

This wasn't an ending, but a new beginning.

A sliver of pure hope pushed down his overwhelming despair and the darkness in his heart. Yes... It had to be. The shaking blade in his hand and the agony it brought was proof. Morrowil was giving him a second chance...He might not be able to stop the rising darkness, but a new generation might, a new hero.

Like a new dawn shining out of the darkness of the last years—a terrible nightmare he didn't know how to save, how to escape, he knew now there was another way...

More importantly, he knew what he had to do. His tendons strained beneath the blade's weight as he stepped forward, dragging Morrowil. Its tip scraped the scorched marble as he reached the edge of the Hall of Wind. At last he stopped, standing upon the precipice. Zephyrs flowed around his body as he looked over the ledge. Far below he glimpsed the city of Morrow. He turned to see the remaining Ronin surrounding him, gripping their blades.

"Why?" Maris asked, emotion racking his voice. He gripped Masamune tightly. He stood over Omni, tears in his eyes. "Why did you do it? What in the seven hells of Remwar have you done to us?"

Kail was silent. No words would suffice. Instead, he looked to her...

Omni lay motionless. Agony, not from the sword, spiraled through him. Her cloth mask had tumbled free in the clash and now her blond hair lay tousled on the white marble. Her beautiful features were tarnished by the streak of scarlet blood running down her temple and matting her hair. *What have I done?* Had it been him? Or the man consumed by his need, his greed for power to heal the world? Omni. He reached out and the other Ronin immediately drew blades, stopping him before he could get closer.

Slowly he nodded, letting his hand drop, though it didn't relieve the tension in the room.

The dignitaries fell from his grasp, choking and gasping on the ground. Some stared in disbelief, while most scrambled to flee the room and the madman who had turned on his own brothers and sister. The madman who had broken the world.

Kail didn't care.

Omni. His heart broke staring at her... His friend, his companion, his greatest ally. What he wouldn't give to see her smile right now, to hear her chide him one last time. As he staggered back, he saw her chest rise and fall—she was alive. That was good. But it was still too late for him, for the Ronin. Though not too late for the next generation. They would fix it all. They would end the darkness. He had only to put the blade in the right hands, to set the wheel in motion for the next chapter.

Kail's foot scraped back, closer to the edge. He put a hand to the marble pillar, teetering.

"Wait!" Maris shouted. Slowly, he rose from Omni's body and moved to Kail. "Just—don't—move." His friend edged closer, dropping his blade and reaching out his arm. "Take it!"

Kail smiled, though the wind now raged angrily around him, threatening to pull him off. "Forgive me."

"Don't," Hiron whispered, lowering his twin blades as well, along with the others. "It wasn't you. It was the blade. We can see that now. You don't have to do this..."

"It doesn't matter," Kail said. "It was still me, my need for power to end this war. I have brought about our end."

Then he saw something...

One of the pedestals holding the stones had been broken, and the tempered glass had been shattered in the battle. Now the sunstone sat in the open, crackling with power. Ophelia's words returned to him.

"He finds the Objects of his desire..." Objects of his desire.... The words teased him until now. The sunstone crackled, light bursting from its core, as if in answer.

It all made sense. Why he wanted them, Kail could only imagine, but it was clear—he must never find them. Just then, Omni groaned, cracking open her gaze. Still too weak to move, she looked at him through blurry eyes. *Kail?* She sent through the bond. *Wh-what are you doing?*

He wants the stones, Omni. I don't know why, but he is coming for them.

Omni looked to the crackling sun orb and light of recognition dawned on her. Then she saw his teetering position. *Then we will hide them. You don't need to do this,* she sent.

I do, he told her. *A darkness has festered inside me. Same as inside Ophelia. I don't know what it is exactly. If it is magic or simply the evil inside all men's hearts, but it prays on fear, on weakness. I can feel it in my veins even now.* Kail looked down and saw a jet-black darkness slithering through his veins and he shook his head. It whispered, begging

29

him to use it, to give in to the dark hunger. *Like a spike in my brain—turning me mad—*

Fight it, Omni demanded through the bond. *If anyone can, it's you!*

I am, but when I break, for it is only a matter of time—I don't know what I'll do... who I'll hurt next.

We are not without defense.

Kail shook his head sadly. She wasn't understanding. Even lying there, wounded, time slowing for them, she was trying to pull him back into the light. *It's much bigger than that, Omni. Morrowil has abandoned me.* Then he smiled at her, despite the darkness, the wind, the pain in his heart. *If it has abandoned me though, that means one thing—*

—It seeks another, Omni finished for him. *A new generation...*

Kail's smile grew. *The Ronin will return. I can only hope they have the strength to do what's right. I'm afraid the others won't understand, but you will. You always do what's necessary.*

It is too late then.... For us... for this age... Omni asked. *Hope is lost.*

Every age has its heroes, Kail answered. *Hope is never lost.*

Then what can we do? She asked, desperately through the bond, as he teetered on the edge. *Tell me.*

Kail looked to the orbs. *Hide them. No matter the costs. Find a way so he can never get them. I don't know what he's planning, or who the evil is, but if he obtains those orbs, something tells me... there will be no redemption for Farhaven. This way... this way we still have a chance. Do this, and all is not lost.*

Why me? She asked, as the other Ronin shouted at him, trying to pull him away from the ledge, but all that mattered in that moment was Omni, lying there. Hair strewn across her face from the winds, her bright blue eyes fixed upon him.

With a small laugh, Kail answered, *That is easy. Because you are stronger than I ever was, and you will make a better leader too. Just perhaps a tad less stubborn.*

Tears filled Omni's eyes as she reached out. *Don't go. We need you... I... I need you.*

Kail smiled sadly. *I believe, my dear friend, that is the first lie you have ever uttered to me,* he sent, then shut the bond and whispered to her, "Goodbye."

Maris was shouting over the sound of rushing wind. "Take my hand, damnit! We can find a way. We always do! It doesn't have to end here!"

"No," Kail said with a glimmer of a smile despite the sorrow in his heart, "No it doesn't. This is an end, but it it is not *the* end. I don't know where this war will end, but I will make it right."

He slipped one foot over the edge and Maris shouted, "Damnit, Kail! Dicing hells, please... just take my hand!" The Ronin of leaf edged closer, extending his shaking palm.

"I speak for all of us, brother—don't," Baro said.

Kail took in each of their faces one last time, etching their faces into his memory. Aundevoria's face was grave as stone like his moniker, his brown eyes and dark skin pinched, yet it was from a pained expression as he stood over his brother. Aurelious, the Ronin of flesh, was clutching a wound on his abdomen that was already pink and whole. Aurelious, hook-nosed, and ebony-skinned like his brother, was looking to Kail with equal worry. Hiron, Ronin of Water, with his fall of straight blond hair and smooth features, and tilt to his bright blue eyes sheathed his dual blades. "Baro's right, Kail. You are not your darkness. Let us fix this, together."

Even Dared, wrapped in black cloth, stepped out of the shadows as Kail's foot slid back. The pained expression on his normally aloof, hooded features spoke volumes. They were still afraid of him, but that little bit warmed Kail's frigid heart.

Still, he knew what he had to do. "Not this time, I'm afraid. We will find each other again, brothers... in this realm or the next. I swear it." With that, Kail let go of the pillar and leaned back.

"No!" Maris cried, lunging forward. A thick vine that had been decoratively wrapped around a marble pillar shot out. It clasped Kail's wrist, holding him in place.

With the last of his strength, Kail lifted Morrowil."Sorry, brother. It's time for me to play the fool hero for once," he said and cut the vine. Their powers reached out for him, but Kail wove threads of wind like a hardened shield. More shards of ice, vine and stone crashed against the barricade uselessly. Wind embraced him as he plummeted, gaining speed, until it raged in his ears. He fell endlessly. The world panned out before him—the vast cliff face of Ren Nar rushing by him, and the ground rushing ever closer.

Kail closed his eyes, embracing his power.

Like the birds he admired, he felt light and free—boundless for the first time.

THE END

Made in the USA
Columbia, SC
17 February 2023

12567057R00026